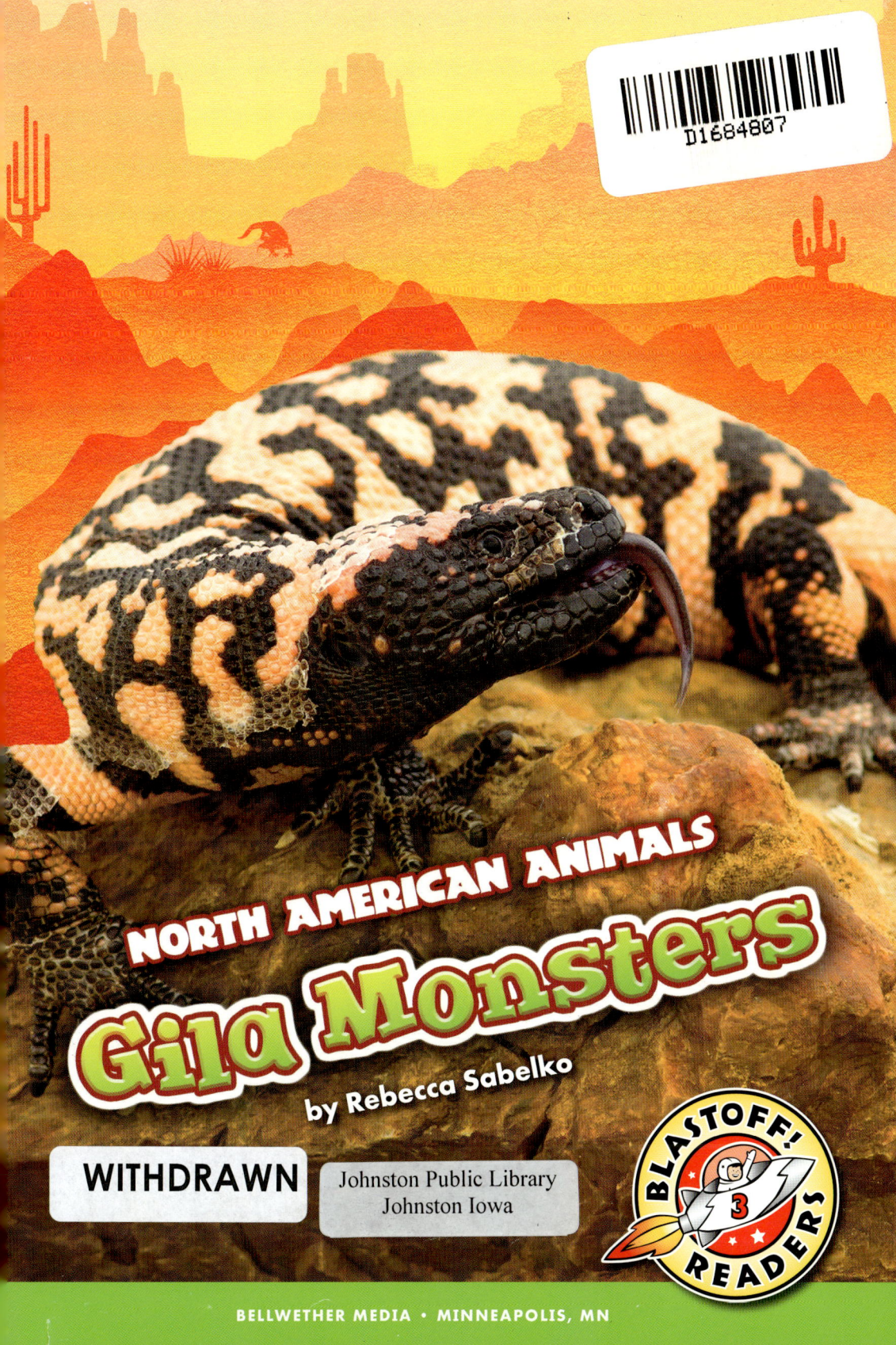

NORTH AMERICAN ANIMALS
Gila Monsters

by Rebecca Sabelko

Note to Librarians, Teachers, and Parents:

Blastoff! Readers are carefully developed by literacy experts and combine standards-based content with developmentally appropriate text.

Level 1 provides the most support through repetition of high-frequency words, light text, predictable sentence patterns, and strong visual support.

Level 2 offers early readers a bit more challenge through varied simple sentences, increased text load, and less repetition of high-frequency words.

Level 3 advances early-fluent readers toward fluency through increased text and concept load, less reliance on visuals, longer sentences, and more literary language.

Level 4 builds reading stamina by providing more text per page, increased use of punctuation, greater variation in sentence patterns, and increasingly challenging vocabulary.

Level 5 encourages children to move from "learning to read" to "reading to learn" by providing even more text, varied writing styles, and less familiar topics.

Whichever book is right for your reader, Blastoff! Readers are the perfect books to build confidence and encourage a love of reading that will last a lifetime!

This edition first published in 2019 by Bellwether Media, Inc.

No part of this publication may be reproduced in whole or in part without written permission of the publisher. For information regarding permission, write to Bellwether Media, Inc., Attention: Permissions Department, 6012 Blue Circle Drive, Minnetonka, MN 55343.

Library of Congress Cataloging-in-Publication Data

Names: Sabelko, Rebecca, author.
Title: Gila Monsters / by Rebecca Sabelko.
Description: Minneapolis, MN : Bellwether Media, Inc., 2019. | Series: Blastoff! Readers. North American Animals | Audience: Age 5-8. | Audience: Grade K to 3. | Includes bibliographical references and index.
Identifiers: LCCN 2017056261 (print) | LCCN 2018004966 (ebook) | ISBN 9781626177970 (hardcover : alk. paper) | ISBN 9781681035222 (ebook)
Subjects: LCSH: Gila monster–North America–Juvenile literature.
Classification: LCC QL666.L247 (ebook) | LCC QL666.L247 S23 2019 (print) | DDC 597.95/952-dc23
LC record available at https://lccn.loc.gov/2017056261

Text copyright © 2019 by Bellwether Media, Inc. BLASTOFF! READERS and associated logos are trademarks and/or registered trademarks of Bellwether Media, Inc. SCHOLASTIC, CHILDREN'S PRESS, and associated logos are trademarks and/or registered trademarks of Scholastic Inc., 557 Broadway, New York, NY 10012.

Editor: Betsy Rathburn   Designer: Josh Brink

Printed in the United States of America, North Mankato, MN.

Table of Contents

What Are Gila Monsters?	4
Built to Dig	8
Plump Tails	14
Mini Monsters	18
Glossary	22
To Learn More	23
Index	24

What Are Gila Monsters?

Gila monsters are one of only two **venomous** lizards in North America! These **reptiles** are named after Arizona's Gila River.

In the Wild

N W E S

Extinct
Extinct in the Wild
Critically Endangered
Endangered
Vulnerable
► Near Threatened ◄
Least Concern

Gila monster range = ▮
conservation status: near threatened

They soak up the sun in the deserts of the southwestern United States. They are also found in northern Mexico.

Gila monsters are not as scary as their name sounds. They move their large bodies slowly.

Much of their time is spent in **burrows**. These help them **hibernate** in the winter and keep cool in the summer.

burrow

Built to Dig

scales

Gilas have beadlike **scales**. These are black with pink or yellow bands along their backs.

Their bodies can reach over 20 inches (51 centimeters) long. But they only weigh about 2 to 4 pounds (0.9 to 2 kilograms).

Gilas have short, powerful legs. They use these to dig burrows and find food.

These reptiles smell using their tongues. They search for **prey** by poking their tongues in and out of their mouths.

Gila monsters have powerful jaws lined with **grooved** teeth. These are most often used against **predators**.

Animals to Avoid

coyotes

Cooper's hawks

roadrunners

mountain lions

Gilas bite down hard if **threatened**. The grooves of their teeth drip **venom** into their enemies.

Plump Tails

These **carnivores** only need three or four meals each year. Some can eat more than 1 pound (0.45 kilograms) of food at once!

Identify a Gila Monster

fat tail   beadlike scales   powerful legs

They store what they eat as fat in their tails. It is time to eat again when their tails get thin!

Gila monsters eat small animals and bugs. They also eat bird and reptile eggs.

Gilas hunt mostly in the morning or as night falls. This helps them escape the desert heat.

Mini Monsters

Gila monsters hibernate all winter. They come out of their burrows once spring arrives. They begin building up their fatty tails.

Soon, females dig nests in the sand. They lay 2 to 15 leathery eggs.

hatchling

The eggs spend the winter underground. Then the **hatchlings** break from their shells. The babies are on their own as soon as they **hatch**. They head off to find their first meal!

Baby Facts

Name for babies: hatchlings

Number of eggs laid: 2 to 15 eggs

Time spent inside egg: 120 to 150 days

Time spent with mom: 1 day

Glossary

burrows—holes or tunnels that some animals dig for homes

carnivores—animals that only eat meat

grooved—marked by narrow channels in the surface

hatch—to break out of an egg

hatchlings—baby Gila monsters

hibernate—to spend the winter sleeping or resting

predators—animals that hunt other animals for food

prey—animals that are hunted by other animals for food

reptiles—cold-blooded animals that have backbones and lay eggs

scales—small plates of skin that cover and protect a Gila monster's body

threatened—in danger

venom—poison created by Gila monsters

venomous—having or producing venom, a poison created by Gila monsters

To Learn More

AT THE LIBRARY

Bernhardt, Carolyn. *Gila Monster: Venomous Desert Dweller*. Minneapolis, Minn.: Checkerboard Library, 2017.

Brett, Flora. *Get to Know Gila Monsters*. North Mankato, Minn.: Capstone Press, 2015.

Phillips, Dee. *Gila Monster's Burrow*. New York, N.Y.: Bearport Publishing, 2015.

ON THE WEB

Learning more about Gila monsters is as easy as 1, 2, 3.

1. Go to www.factsurfer.com.

2. Enter "Gila monsters" into the search box.

3. Click the "Surf" button and you will see a list of related web sites.

With factsurfer.com, finding more information is just a click away.

Index

Arizona, 4
bodies, 6, 9
burrows, 7, 10, 18
carnivores, 14
colors, 8
deserts, 5, 17
dig, 10, 19
eggs, 16, 19, 20, 21
females, 19
food, 10, 14, 16, 17
Gila River, 4
hatch, 20
hatchlings, 20, 21
hibernate, 7, 18
hunt, 17
jaws, 12
legs, 10, 15
Mexico, 5

name, 4, 6
nests, 19
predators, 12, 13
prey, 11, 16, 17
range, 5
reptiles, 4, 11, 16
scales, 8, 15
seasons, 7, 18, 20
size, 6, 9
smell, 11
status, 5
tails, 15, 18
teeth, 12, 13
tongues, 11
United States, 5
venom, 4, 13

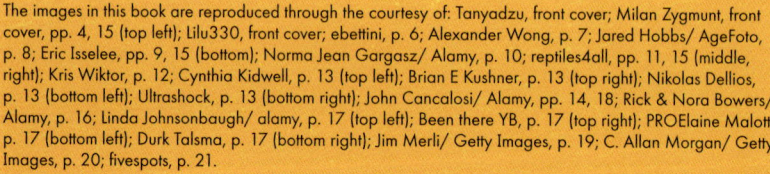

The images in this book are reproduced through the courtesy of: Tanyadzu, front cover; Milan Zygmunt, front cover, pp. 4, 15 (top left); Lilu330, front cover; ebettini, p. 6; Alexander Wong, p. 7; Jared Hobbs/ AgeFoto, p. 8; Eric Isselee, pp. 9, 15 (bottom); Norma Jean Gargasz/ Alamy, p. 10; reptiles4all, pp. 11, 15 (middle, right); Kris Wiktor, p. 12; Cynthia Kidwell, p. 13 (top left); Brian E Kushner, p. 13 (top right); Nikolas Dellios, p. 13 (bottom left); Ultrashock, p. 13 (bottom right); John Cancalosi/ Alamy, pp. 14, 18; Rick & Nora Bowers/ Alamy, p. 16; Linda Johnsonbaugh/ alamy, p. 17 (top left); Been there YB, p. 17 (top right); PROElaine Malott, p. 17 (bottom left); Durk Talsma, p. 17 (bottom right); Jim Merli/ Getty Images, p. 19; C. Allan Morgan/ Getty Images, p. 20; fivespots, p. 21.